to
Georges

Stephanie Blake

NITS!

GECKO PRESS

In Simon's class there's a girl called Lou.

Simon loves Lou.

The trouble is,
Lou loves
Mamadou.

Simon is VERY jealous.

Especially when Mamadou kisses Lou.

One day
Lou begins to itch.
She
has
NITS.
One hundred
million trillion
itchy scratchy
little nits.

Poor
LOU.
Everyone
stares at her.
Even Mamadou,
who chants,
"Lou's got nits!
Lou's got nits!"

Simon
doesn't care.
"I love nits!
I mean,
I love Lou!"

"Don't worry,"
he tells her.
"Your mother
will fix it."

"But Simon
aren't you scared
of nits?"

"No.
I love you
AND your nits!"

Then Lou
gives
Simon
something
very sweet...

A kiss.

And also…

Nits.

This edition first published in 2019 by Gecko Press
PO Box 9335, Marion Square, Wellington 6141, New Zealand
info@geckopress.com

English-language edition © Gecko Press Ltd 2019
Translation © Linda Burgess 2019

Original title: *Poux!*
Text and illustrations by Stephanie Blake
© 2009 l'école des loisirs, Paris

Edited by Penelope Todd
Typesetting by Katrina Duncan
Printed in China by Everbest Printing Co. Ltd,
an accredited ISO 14001 & FSC-certified printer

Hardback ISBN: 978-1-776572-23-6
Paperback ISBN: 978-1-776572-24-3

For more curiously good books, visit www.geckopress.com